It was Christmas-time and Thomas was
pulling Annie and Clarabel home
full of people with their shopping.

Among the passengers was a woman with a large basket on her knees.

"It's my cat, Timmy," she said, and she opened the basket a little way to show the other passengers.

Timmy thought he was being set free
and he wriggled out of the basket,
jumped onto the seat, out of the window
and vanished into the snow.

At the station all the passengers got out of the train and helped to look for him. The guard and the stationmaster helped too, but Timmy was nowhere to be found.

Meanwhile, Thomas had other things to worry about.
He had run out of water, but the water-column was frozen.
"We'll fill your tanks with snow," said his driver.

Thomas's tanks were almost full,
when a shovelful of snow made a
funny squeaky noise and began to move.

Yes, it was the lost cat,
very wet and very cold.
The stationmaster dried it and
his wife gave it a saucer of milk.

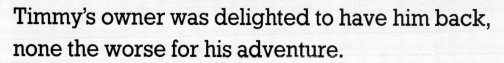

Timmy's owner was delighted to have him back,
none the worse for his adventure.
She put him in the basket and firmly secured the lid.
"Thank you, Thomas," she said. "Happy Christmas, everyone."
"Miaow," said the basket.

Published by Kaye & Ward,
an imprint of William Heinemann Ltd
Michelin House, 81 Fulham Road
London SW3 6RB
© 1988 William Heinemann Ltd

Reprinted 1988

ISBN 0 434 92740 6
Printed in Hong Kong by Mandarin Offset